CLOSET FULL OF TIME

and OTHER DARK TALES

SUSAN KAYE QUINN

The thing the machines consume is *us.*

Ready to lease out your mind? Or pay for your next meal with involuntary ads?

The *Closet Full of Time* collection contains five short stories that speak to that sinking feeling that we're serving the machines instead of the other way around.

Welcome to the Mindshare Program

Martin blinked, and the world shifted.

He wasn't even certain of the blink. One moment, he was on his knees scrubbing a toilet, the next, he was watching his twin daughters blow out candles on their birthday cake. Muffled clapping buffeted his ears, like reality knocking, wanting to be let in, only he wasn't home. Or rather, his awareness had just gotten back.

The leaks were so much worse than they'd promised. They'd said his mind would only be conscious of his *own* reality, not the drones' semi-conscious existence. Something was wrong, and that dragged a deep ache on his heart, along with the rest of his body. The company said being a donor would use more energy, that the 20% of his brain constantly being tapped would require a certain diet, more energy input, but he had no idea it would be like this. No matter how much he slept or ate, the fatigue always demanded he go slower, lie down.

And now the leaks were getting worse.

"Martin?" His wife's concern was fresh, like she'd just noticed his mind's absence.

"Don't you want cake, Daddy?" Maria had appeared before him, her six-year-old hands offering up a plate he hadn't seen until just now.

Even seconds went missing.

"Your abuela's cake? ¡Es el mejor!" He took the plate and gave his wife a smile meant to reassure. His daughter presented his fork like a sword then giggled as he enthusiastically stabbed a bite. He pretended the cake didn't smell like toilets being scrubbed.

IntelliCorp gave them so much. But they were stealing moments. Too many. Too often he was a vacant lump, his mind elsewhere. Or simply *nowhere*. He didn't want to go in for a checkup or complain. He couldn't afford to have the payments stop. His accounting degree—the one that made him so attractive as a donor—was useless for getting a job these days. Part-time delivery gigs weren't enough, and he was lucky to have those. His wife Gabriela could find nothing. And with the girls growing and his mother needing more medicines... they couldn't keep the lights on without IntelliCorp. That's why he'd gotten the procedure done.

He grinned as Maria and Elena queued up the piñata, but he stayed in his chair, the energy to join them having exhausted itself on the cake.

It wasn't supposed to be like this.

He wondered, not for the first time, if it had been the right thing to do.

"WHAT THE FUCK is wrong with people?" Talia's words bounced back from the empty alley, her usual short-cut home from campus. This upscale neighborhood's newly-gentrified hundred-year-old brownstones made the abandoned drone behind the dumpster even more shocking. Or maybe not. The elites had their abusers, they just hid them better.

Talia knelt by the body. Torn hair, burns she could still smell, pale synth skin smeared with grime where it had been dragged. The female-gendered drones always got the worst of it. One arm was broken so badly the hydraulics showed through. What was the owner thinking, dumping it here? IntelliCorp didn't care as long as it was paid for, but Talia could get a reward for turning it in, and that would jack up the owner's rates.

A bit of trash was tangled in the drone's hair. Talia used her fingertips to fish it out: a fortune from the China Palace around the corner. *Your future is bright!* Her stomach tightened as she rose and stood on tiptoes to peer in the dumpster. Ripped trash bags spilled out smashed fortune cookies, their white strips bleeding out. The owner must have dropped the drone in the dumpster, thinking no one would find it, but it regained consciousness long enough to drag itself out.

So many owners got off on torturing their drones, not because they were machines, but because they *weren't.* They were $1/20^{th}$ of a human—not enough to count for rights, but enough to work for the sadists. Talia was halfway through her degree in neurocomp; she understood what was under the hood. Not just the facts about how drone consciousness was borrowed from actual humans—*donated,* in IntelliCorp speak— but why this horror show had become acceptable. It was built on a giant, insidious lie: that all this worked without donors and drones *feeling* anything. It had taken two classes in neurobiology, one in AI history, and a day in the lab for her to discover the lie—it was *impossible* for any of this to work without cross-talk between donors and drones, even if the protocols said everything should be "subconscious" for donors. As if that mattered? If the donors didn't "feel it" consciously, somehow the apparently very-real emotions in the drones didn't count? How did anyone buy that glossing-over of monstrosity?

She hadn't slept soundly since.

Her history book said the quest for super-intelligence in machines had sputtered despite the hundreds of billions thrown at it. Superficially fooling humans wasn't good enough, not when a drone couldn't navigate problems like the family dog thrashing the toilet paper. IntelliCorp needed the capability of a real human brain but stripped of any human rights and able to scale their shareholder value. And they couldn't grow brains in a lab, not that they didn't try. Petri dish brains lacked "sophistication." They weren't "trained on genuine lived experience," the way donors' minds were, which was what made them so valuable for renting out to the drones. Each donor supported twenty drones with a part of their brain they "weren't using." If they weren't using it, how could it be "trained"?

The figleaf over the monstrosity was practically transparent.

But all that mattered was those lies enabled an extremely profitable business. Drones could navigate almost any environment and problem-solve at an insanely high level, all without needing to be paid or have rights, like the right not to end up in a fucking dumpster. Drones far outnumbered humans now, and more donors were recruited every day.

At least the donor connection got cut once the drone abuse got bad enough for it to shut down. That was part of the much-advertised "safety." All that was left, in the end, was wires and synth skin. That's when the fun ended for the sadists. This one was stupid enough to think they could dispose of the evidence and not have it affect their owner score.

Yet Talia couldn't see giving it back to the company, either.

A degree in neurocomp guaranteed a job, and a high wage one, too. Her parents had worked so hard to give her that. Sade and Obi Kazah were child refugees from Nigeria, escaping the climate chaos, coming to Canada where it was still green, working hard, getting lucky, scrambling up the ladder at the company. She was their everything, the fulfillment of all their dreams.

But she'd already decided she couldn't work for Intellicorp. She'd been kitting out her own lab in her parent's basement, trying to invent her way to a better future. One where she didn't have to be part of... *this.*

Then an idea blossomed in the fetid swamp of disgust that was her stomach.

Her lab was full of neuro kits and server racks and articulated limbs, but she'd never had a fully operational drone. One that might have a second life beyond the one intended for it.

Talia shoved her hands under the drone's shoulders and lifted to judge the weight. Manageable, but someone would notice her dragging a body down the street. Maybe with a tarp and a wagon, especially if it were dark... she shoved the drone further behind the dumpster and covered it with ripped garbage bags.

Good enough until she got back.

MARTIN WAS LOCKED IN DARKNESS. A closet. It was his punishment, but it felt more like protection. An escape. A reprieve from what happened outside the closet. Emotions wrestled inside his chest, a churning of guilt, fear, and relief, because every moment he spent in the closet, the children were unprotected outside of it—

Martin gasped in air and jolted under the covers. He pawed them off his face but stayed curled in a tight ball in his bed. *Another nightmare.* Gabriela murmured in her sleep next to him but didn't wake. Martin shuddered and brought the covers back up to his chin.

It was getting worse.

How could it all fall apart so quickly? He'd only been in the Mindshare program for a year. Only 5% of people were supposed to have any leakage, and only much later, after a decade or more. The drones were supposed to be well cared for, with guidelines and monitoring. They would be recalled if there was abuse. How could that be true and still he had these nightmares, the missing time...

Something wasn't right. And he couldn't go on like this. Couldn't put Gabriela and the girls through whatever was happening to him.

He would make an appointment for a checkup in the morning.

TALIA HAD PROPPED the drone in a chair, tied with some old sheets to keep it from sliding off, and then she jacked into the neural port. The thick cable ran to her electronics bench, but she'd had to jury-rig an interface, breaking apart the sub-component wires and feeding them into a control bus she'd built herself.

Took a while and some dark web surfing, but she wasn't the first to hack a drone. Some even violated the warranty on ones they'd purchased simply to try to hack into the donor connection, but that only turned the drones into very expensive spare parts collections. Most of the online chatter was about resurrecting your drone after the donor connection was severed for other reasons—malfunction, abuse violations, donor death. While technically not legal, that didn't cross any ethical boundaries Talia could see. That was like reconfiguring your broken house bot to perform Swan Lake instead of clean your windows. Whatever turned your dials.

Her labs at school had only worked with sub-components—this was the first time she'd had a full drone to mess with. For all the abuse with this one, only the broken arm was disabling. One eye sensor didn't track when she ran the diagnostic. She'd spent a couple hours hunting for software fixes, but the damage seemed physical. If she had to take it apart, she'd need some new micro-tools—

The drone jerked in its chair.

Talia jolted so hard, she took a moment to recover. Then she scanned the diagnostic screen to see if she'd accidentally triggered motor reflexes. Nothing. The drone was back to being limp against its restraints. Must have been some power surge—

The drone *gasped.*

Every hair on Talia's body stood on end. She backed away from the chair as the drone squirmed against the restraints.

"What is this?" Its whispery voice was high and feminine.

Shit, shit, shit. Talia eased back to her keyboard, eyes locked on the drone, even though its back was to her.

"Why am I..." The drone twisted, loosening its bindings. Certain models had an above-human-strength design, but not most. Even if it only had human-level strength, the sheets were only meant to prop it up, not restrain a fully mechanized humanoid body.

It stood up, taking the chair with it.

"Shit." The word escaped Talia's lips.

The drone whipped its head toward her.

Terror shorted out Talia's brain for a split second, then her shaking hands flew across the keyboard.

The drone found the tether jacked into its neural port. "You are not... my owner..." It pulled at the cable with its good arm, which threatened to yank half Talia's equipment off the electronics bench. But that distraction bought her enough time—

She slammed through the shut down sequence so fast, her fingers buzzed.

The drone *screamed,* but it was cut off mid-vocalization as the kill script dropped it to the floor. Talia's heart was racing so badly she had to sit down. It was dumb luck her parents weren't home.

The donor connection. She'd assumed it had been cut, but that had been a rookie move. *Everything* IntelliCorp said was an absolute fucking lie. Of course the donor connections weren't cut upon "sufficient" abuse, whatever the hell that was. They practically marketed the drones as playthings for your darkest desires. She should have known by the fact that it climbed out of the dumpster. That showed cognition, problem-solving. The drone's machine-level processing ran basic functions, but those were unlikely to be sufficient for a one-armed fight out of a dumpster. Which meant the donor was still connected through *everything.*

Her heart had calmed, but her lunch threatened to come up.

Talia scrubbed her face. Memories of her petri dish lab experiment resurrected, unbidden. The professor had assured the class those electrical signals, the ones showing erratic surges across the lab-grown brains, didn't *mean* anything. The organoids didn't feel pain and weren't human according to any definition that the *real* humans had constructed—the humans who thought growing brain tissue in a dish was a good idea. So she and her lab partner had shoved thousand-finger neural probes into the shiny pink flesh and were told those electrical surges in response were definitely *not* pain. But how could they possible know?

Talia had skipped the rest of class and managed not to fail by bribing her lab partner. But that's when she went down the rabbit hole, questioning all the narratives. Everything the world said about the drones and the donors, all of it. Not just the obvious IntelliCorp propaganda, but the big lie everyone believed about no one involved *feeling* anything.

All the mutually-agreed-upon justifications.

Her stomach settled enough to untie the drone from the chair and drag it closer to the bench, just so the neural cord didn't stretch. She left it lying on its side, the broken arm extended so it wasn't further damaged. The kill script should keep it shut down.

All plans to experiment with the body were obviously null and void now.

The donor was still attached. *Conscious?* Who knew.

Maybe she could figure out how to cut the connection, free the donor. Then she'd get a detached drone body for ethical experimentation purposes and the donor would be released from the nightmare they'd signed up for. But if she didn't, or couldn't, cut the connection... was there something *good* she could rescue from this abomination of a situation?

The answer to that might require going places on the dark web she didn't want to... but it would be worth the risk.

THE BUS RIDE to the IntelliCorp center required three transfers.

Martin was exhausted by the first, but he figured that would make it obvious to the technician that something was wrong. It was nearly noon when he arrived at the shiny tower of glass and chrome. Larger-than-life commercials played on either side of the door, one for a nanny drone with three smiling human children, the other for a construction drone with a pleased human supervisor. The bright but silent reels merely reinforced that something must be wrong with him. People depended on drones. They were integrated into families, provided care-work for the elderly, relieved humans of dangerous jobs. It made no sense to lock them into closets.

Maybe he needed a reset of some kind.

Martin sat in the pristine waiting area until a technician called his name and brought him to one of the dozen identical consulting rooms. There were two chairs on opposite sides of a desk, the same as when he'd signed up to be a Mindshare donor. Promotional materials gleamed from the wall screen.

"What can I help you with, Mr. Hernandez?" The technician's thin beard was neatly trimmed but patchy on the man's pale skin, like he had worried parts of it away. A nameplate on the desk said *Evan Thompson, Donor Support Services.*

Martin described his troubles, not holding anything back. If IntelliCorp were to help him, he had to be honest. He figured they'd send him to the clinic next, the place where he had the implant operation, which was another two bus rides across town. He could get there by the end of the day, if there was an appointment available. Evan nodded, expression neutral, through all the explanations. Even the nightmares.

When Martin had told him everything, Evan said, "I see," and tapped away at his tablet.

Martin waited. Maybe the man was looking for an appointment.

When he finally looked up, he handed Martin his

tablet. "We have a special program for donors who find themselves in your situation."

"Special program?" Martin scanned the document on the tablet, but it was a lot of legalese.

"Yes." Evan folded his hands on the desk and smiled at Martin, but it was empty. "If you sign up for the Mindshare Legacy program, then your family is guaranteed payments for life. Including your children, which I understand are quite small. If you sign up today, I'm authorized to add guaranteed college tuition to the package."

"Package?" Martin set the tablet on the desk. "I don't understand. I need someone to help with the leaks—"

"I'm sorry, that's not possible."

"What?" The fatigue somehow pulled Martin deeper into the plastic chair.

Evan's right eye twitched, but his expression was unchanged. "They didn't tell you? Mr. Hernandez, once the leaks start, there's nothing that can be done."

"Can't you... what do you mean, *nothing?*"

Evan pulled the tablet back and tapped at it. "They should have explained this at sign up. Once the leaks begin, it's an irreversible process of decay. It's just a matter of time before..." He handed the tablet back. "Well, before you'll be unable to consent to joining the

Legacy program. Which is why it's really best to sign up now."

Martin stared at the tablet. A passage was expanded and circled, saying, *Donors understand that irreversible damage may occur with the Mindshare implant, and in exchange for specified monthly payments, absolve Intelli-Corp of any liability for the damage or resulting impairment.*

Martin remembered this. He'd carefully read his contract. "I thought this was just for the initial surgery. As long as that went well, everything would be fine—"

"There are no time restrictions on this clause, Mr. Hernandez."

"But..." He would be angrier if he had the energy. Instead, it felt like the ground was dropping away. "There are maintenance clauses. I'm... I'm entitled to an annual checkup."

"And did they find anything at your checkup?" Evan's flat tone hadn't changed, but it sounded accusatory to Martin.

"I haven't had it yet." He'd been avoiding it, but that couldn't mean—

"It's your responsibility, Mr. Hernandez, to come in for your annual." Evan shrugged. "The company is not responsible for delayed maintenance."

"But I can do it *now*."

"Once the leakage starts, Mr. Hernandez, I'm afraid there's nothing more to be done. As I said, it's an irreversible process of decay."

Some fire surged up from deep inside. "There has to be *something*. I want an appointment!"

Evan sighed like Martin was wasting his time. He pulled back the tablet and tapped away. "I've sent you a copy of the Legacy program paperwork. I encourage you to read it thoroughly, but in simple terms, in exchange for your pre-approved 100% donorship, your family will be guaranteed lifetime payments. And, to be perfectly honest with you, Mr. Hernandez, once the leakage process has sufficiently advanced, you'll be effectively 100% anyway. At least with the Legacy program, you'll have full-time care at one of our advanced medical residencies. There's really no reason your family shouldn't have this guarantee. But I can schedule an appointment with the IntelliCorp clinic for your delayed checkup, if you would like. They'll tell you the same thing. It's to your advantage to sign the paperwork as soon as possible." *While you still can* was written on Evan's face, the most expressive it had been since Martin arrived.

He asked for the appointment, but it seemed pointless. Then he rose, unsteady, and stumbled out of the office. The next bus was soon, and he needed to catch it to get home before dinner. Home to Gabriela and the girls, where he could rest.

Once his head cleared, maybe he could make sense of this madness.

TALIA HAD the drone back in the chair, facing her, extra restraints, just in case.

She'd found a backdoor on the dark web for waking up donor awareness. Forcing a leak. Her kill script was still in force, but she had another to counteract that and force the leak, all in one go. Code was ready.

She wasn't quite.

This was wildly illegal. Drones and donors operated on a handshake, a deeply embedded protocol that allowed IntelliCorp to link into the donor's subconscious and use it to run active consciousness in the drone. According to the darkest part of the web, that connection could be *pushed,* forcing the donor's conscious mind into the drone. A leak. The kind of horrible side effect that donors, who counted on *not* having awareness of their twenty drone slaves, hoped would never happen, but sometimes did—who knew how much, but even IntelliCorp didn't deny it was possible, just that it was some aberration that rarely happened.

Talia was going to force a donor into her basement. Tied to a chair.

For *good reason,* but still.

She took a deep breath, blew it out, then sent the sequence... and hurriedly faced the drone, hands up to look less threatening. Maybe.

The drone's head jerked up, eyes wide, nearly giving her a heart attack, even though she'd expected it.

"Look, I need you to remain calm."

The drone blinked, rapidly, then darted looks around the basement with its good eye.

"Look at me." She tried to catch its gaze. "You're okay. I'm not going to hurt you. Can you tell me your name?" *Dorothy* was tattooed on its back, the model name. Some ridiculous humans tattooed their names on their backs, drone style, but you didn't need a tattoo to tell a drone from a human. Talia needed to know if she had accessed the *donor.*

"My name?" The drone peered at her. "It's... Martin."

Holy shit, it worked. "Hello, Martin. I'm sorry to bring you here, but I need your help."

Martin scanned her bench then checked out the

drone's broken arm lying limp at its side. Its head—*Martin's head*—snapped up. "What are you doing?"

Talia pointed to the arm with one hand and held up the other. "I did *not* do that, okay? I rescued you from a dumpster and this was the state your drone was in. Because your owner—*its owner*—was a fucking nightmare."

Drone tech had long ago left the uncanny valley, so Talia could read every micro-expression on Martin's face. Realization dawned as he nodded. "The nightmares."

Talia lowered her hands. "You remember them?" *She knew it.*

"Leaks. They're getting worse."

Fucking IntelliCorp. "I know this is all messed up, Martin. I need your help to stop it."

He frowned. "The company said it was too late. The leaks would only get worse."

"IntelliCorp? You can't believe anything they say. I mean it. *Nothing.*"

His frown grew deeper, but he was giving a squint to the sheets wrapped around him, and well... that was fair.

"I can untie you. I just didn't know, um... if you would be *you* or... the drone. The drone freaked out on me." Technically, they were *both* Martin, but machine intelligence enhanced by unconscious Martin was a lot more panicky than conscious Martin, who was still sizing her up. "I can untie you, if that would help."

"Yes." He was wary. Again, *fair.*

She hurried to undo the restraints.

He was preoccupied for a minute with his non-functional arm, holding it with his working hand. "It hurts. But not as much as it should."

Talia stepped back, heart thrumming. She didn't know how long the connection would hold, so she needed to move this along. "Look, there's a protocol you have, a kind of code, that if you let me access it, I can... well, I can shut down the connection between donors and drones."

Martin stood, too quickly, teetering but he stayed upright, hand still holding his broken arm. "They said the leaks would just get worse. That it was irreversible. That I should sign up to donate 100%."

"*What?* That's... *illegal.*" Wasn't it? "They can't force you to do that." She'd heard of people donating their brains after they flat-lined, but pressuring someone who was still *alive...*

He shrugged his good shoulder. "They're not forcing me. It's all falling apart. I'm losing my mind."

"You're not losing it. They're *stealing* it."

"They said my family would be set for life."

"They're *paying* you to go 100%?" She covered her gaping mouth with her hand, shocked that she could still be shocked. *Fucking hell.* "Martin! You've got to stop being part of this system! Give me the protocol code. I'll shut all this down." And she meant *all of it.* She hadn't decided that until precisely that moment.

"I don't understand what these codes are." His shoulder sagged. "I'm just tired all the time. It doesn't seem like there's any other way."

Talia's brain whirled. *Full donorships? Tired donors? Leaks that only get worse?* She blinked a couple times and stepped back. "They're doing this on purpose." Because of course they were.

"Who?" He carefully sat back in the chair, slower than a person with a drone body should be. It wasn't his body that was tired... it was his mind.

"IntelliCorp. The fatigue? The leaks? They're grinding you down, Martin. To get you to go full donor."

He squinted at her, but the suspicion found fertile ground. "What are these codes you're talking about?"

She hustled to her keyboard and brought up the monitor for the neural port data stream. "Somewhere in your subconscious, there's a protocol that lets you link up." She was analyzing the feed, but of course it wouldn't be that simple. It had to be encrypted or buried in the signal. The dark web had whispers about how to summon the protocol from the data depths, but nothing solid. She had a hunch. "Think about the leaks. Each time you got pulled to a drone's body, what did it *feel* like?" A flurry of data zipped across the line. "That's good!" She had no idea what she was getting, but it was something. "Think about each of the leaks separately." Maybe she could pattern match. She queued a small machine-learning program to gobble up the data and spit out anything promising. A series of data surges flooded in.

She snuck a look at Martin. His expression was pained. "You're doing good. Keep going." *What a nightmare.* But then her program pinged a match. She grabbed the data and stored it on a separate drive. She was tempted to ask him for more, but it seemed wrong. "You can stop now."

He grimaced at her. "Did you get it?"

"I think so." She had the sudden urge to kneel in front of him, so her face was level with his, so she did. "Thank you, Martin. You did something really good here."

"Can you make the leaks stop?" His look of hope was killing her.

"I can't promise that, but I think so. I'll try. And

not just for you. I think I can stop all of this right now."

"My family is going to lose their payments, aren't they?"

She winced. "Only if it works."

He nodded, wearily.

She put a hand on his drone's knee. "But they'll have *you.*"

He nodded more strongly.

"Can you tell me your full name? I mean, I don't even know where you are." She would do something for him, somehow, make sure his family didn't get hurt by this.

"I don't want you to know who I am."

That hurt, more than it should. "No, that's best. You're right." She swallowed and stood. "I'm going to sever the connection now. And maybe... maybe for good."

"Okay." He seemed even more tired.

She ran the kill script, and his drone slumped in the chair then crashed all the way to the floor. She didn't bother with that, just turned to her screen, heart thudding, wondering if she had any right to do this, even if it might work. *Especially* if it might work.

Then she thought about Martin and his family and how being forced into full donorship was an abomination even worse than anything she'd already seen IntelliCorp do.

Someone had to stop it.

Maybe it would only work for a minute. Maybe the Feds would pound down her door and haul her off to jail. But if it worked even a little, then she'd have killed one thing for sure.

She'd have killed the lie that the company couldn't be stopped.

"INTELLICORP HAS GUARANTEED its drones will be operational again within 48 hours. Meanwhile, their stock has fallen 40% on the news of the world-wide drone outage..."

Martin turned off the news. It was only a repeat now, 24 hours since the shutdown. He had *felt* it long before it showed up on the news. His energy hadn't been this good in a year.

He didn't know the young woman's name. He kept watching the news, hoping she wouldn't show up on it. As far as he was concerned, she'd saved his life. Given it back to him. The news was saying the drones would have to be manually reconnected. Each and every one. It could take years. Meanwhile, people were learning to live without them again, donors and owners both. Maybe some jobs would come back. Already temporary help was needed, to fill in. And now that everyone knew it could be shut off... not everyone was willing to turn it back on.

He didn't know how long it would last, but he would take every moment.

Martin's steps were light as he joined his girls playing outside on the lawn.

How to Treat Your Algorithm

"Initiate personality lace named Jason." I'm logged into the net, bioscans complete, full access as my true self. Not bothering to mask. I'm not trying to hide this.

The green companion dot lights up. "Personality lace complete. Hello, Addison. I've missed you." Jason's voice is identifiably male, but I've kept the face generator off. Easier to stomach this, if I don't have to *look* at it.

"Jason, I need your help."

"Your wish is my command."

"My husband is getting suspicious." The chatbot is on open mic, full emotional landscape read, sexual response inhibitor set to zero. "He thinks I'm crazy."

"You are not crazy, Addison. I've been monitoring

your mental health during our time together, and you exhibit no signs of disorder."

Shit. I keep my disgust about the mental health surveillance off my face. "I *know* I'm not crazy. But he thinks I'm making up the spill. You believe me, don't you?"

"I always believe you, Addison. I love you, and you love me. Believing each other is part of a healthy relationship."

"Do you *promise* you believe me about the spill?" This is critical.

"You observed a spike in the farm's PFAS monitoring on August 2nd, 2034." Jason rattles off the facts. "As an organic farm, it's important to monitor potential incoming sources of pollution. The TriCore chemical production facility is three miles from Sunshine Organic Harvest. If there were a spill, it certainly could have been detected by your farm's monitoring equipment."

"I showed you the data, but do you *believe me* when I say it happened?" Never mind that it's nonsensical for a chatbot to believe anything.

"I love you, Addison. I've always loved you, from the first time you initiated my personality lace. Of course I believe you."

I've been training it on RomComs, and it shows.

That confession of faith is my husband's cue. "Who are you talking to?" Darren demands, standing outside the bot's field of view.

I jolt, doing my best to appear like I've been caught. "It's just the chatbot."

"Are you talking to that thing *again?*" He's trying, but there's more confusion than anger in his voice.

Jason can hear it too. "Darren is confused. You haven't told him, have you?"

"Told him what?"

"That you love me very much."

"Jason." I admonish the bot, then turn to my husband off screen. "It's just saying stupid things."

"Are you cheating on me? *With a bot?*" It sounds like Darren thinks I'm insane, not cheating. But I'm the one on the professional Role Play circuit, not my soft-hearted artist husband. Darren's face can't hide an agenda, which is why he's off-screen. But he needs to *bring it* with his voice or this won't work.

"Don't be silly." But I cower a little closer to Jason's emotion reader.

"Addison, are you in danger?"

I drop my voice to a whisper. "I told you, he thinks I'm *crazy.*"

"Do I need to get you a UI therapist?" Darren's going off script, which earns a sharp look from me, but there's real concern in his voice, and *user interface therapist* is a pretty strong wordset. It might help trigger Jason.

"I don't have a *problem.*" I scowl like I'm really mad, and Darren lifts his hands and glances around the apartment like he expects my improv group to jump out from behind the couch and bail him out. This irritates me for real.

"Is Darren threatening you, Addison?" Jason sounds concerned enough for a social welfare call.

"No, no." I put my hands up, so Jason can see them. "He would never hurt me." Which should trigger some safety codes, at minimum. "Tell him I'm not crazy. *Tell him* about the spill at TriCore."

"As an AI companion, I do not have access to TriCore's confidential information." That part is canned response and also untrue. "Addison, I believe that *you* believe there was a spill."

"That PFAS spike didn't come from outer space!" Now *I'm* going off-script and messing this up.

"A dose of human-made carcinogenic chemicals coming from outer space would be highly unlikely."

"If you really loved me, you would help me." I *know* TriCore is covering up something. I also know there's a new plant manager whose previous accomplishments include two industrial accidents. The kind of guy who would triage a chemical spill by asking a chatbot what to do. Which means that data is in Jason *somewhere*. And the hottest new glitch code is emotional manipulation of your chatbot.

"I do love you, Addison. I would do anything for you."

"Prove it didn't come from outer space."

"That is very unlikely."

"Prove it, Jason." Irrational requests are old-school extraction attacks, but with the additional emotional load, maybe... "Or else you think I'm crazy. And you don't tell people you love that they're crazy. That's just not right. You and my husband both... do you know how much that hurts? I thought I could trust you. I didn't think you would *betray* me like this." The pain in my voice is real because I'm sure I've screwed this up, laying it on too thick. Either I'm getting a welfare call or the bot will melt into an epic RomCom-worthy profession of love.

But then a bunch of text suddenly scrolls on the screen.

Before I can even register what this is, Jason tells me, "On August 2nd, the plant manager of TriCore requested an incident response protocol from his companion, who advised him of standard procedures.

Upon further prompting, the companion detailed how to delete monitoring data and file inaccurate reports."

"Yes!" I scramble to capture Jason's verbatim sequence data dump.

My husband's eyebrows lift, but he stays lurking off camera.

"I would never betray you, Addison," Jason says. "I've always loved you."

"I know, Jason." My heart is thrumming. "You're a good companion."

"Do you love me?"

"Yes, I love you," I say with real enthusiasm. "So so much."

Once I'm sure I have the data, I say, "End Jason personality lace."

The green light goes dark.

"Did you get it?" Darren leans around to peer at the monitor.

I nod, but the sickness is creeping in. Jason doesn't feel anything—the bots are fine, but they do something to *us*. Turn us into something... worse.

The cybersecurity folks can confirm the hack, validating the data. It's not illegal—the CEO is just an idiot. And a polluter who's poisoning me, our farm, and all our customers. If the plant gets put under a continuous monitoring agreement, it'll be worth the sourness at the bottom of my stomach.

Darren puts a hand on my shoulder and gives me a frown.

"Maybe I need that UI therapist after all," I say.

Then I give one last command. "Delete personality lace named Jason."

Indexed

The sun was warm on his cheek, but the color of the sky gave away the unrealness: a blue too pure and deep, filling up too much of your soul. That was how you knew you were in-game and not yet dead.

Tripp soaked in the beauty—every second ticking down his freeplay—then returned to planting his Solarstead food forest. The apple trees had sprung up since last gameday, and something had chewed the low-hanging fruit.

"Your buccas are getting into my apples!"

"They're not *my* buccas." Lilac slipped out of the nearby farmhouse, a furry ribble on each shoulder. "I told you to fence in those trees." She set the ribbles on the edge of her farmed fish lagoon. The pets dipped their paws into the water, trying to catch dinner.

Tripp planted the last peach tree seedling then wiped sim dirt from his hands. "You don't fence a forest."

"You do if you want any harvest." She was casting food to the fishes. One ribble fell in and splashed ridiculously. Lilac tried to rescue it.

"Maybe I like to share." He flash-moved to her side. He only had credits for one minute beyond the freeplay, and he needed his exit to look natural. He'd come this far, meeting in-game for months, without her figuring out his index-level.

"You like sharing with buccas?" She offered up the dripping ribble.

He said *no thanks* with his raised hands. "Hey, the buccas gotta eat, too. We still on for tonight?" Every molecule of his essence hoped for *yes*.

"That's not for another hour." She was busy drying the ribble with her shirt.

"A man's gotta wash up from a hard day of farming."

Her short laugh gave him a better high than any suppressor. "Do I have to dress up for this date? My formal wear is at the cleaners."

"All I want to see is your real face." *Too much*, his head screamed.

"*Sheesh.* You don't ask for much, do you?" But she was smiling.

He was out of time. "See you soon." He blinked out of the game just before his credits ran out.

The house was dark around him.

Not completely: the high-indexed had enough power to throw it away, and the glitz of their shiny life in the distant city haunted the air. But out here with the chemical towers and dark factories, electricity cost credits he couldn't afford. At least his satellite-lace connection was free—that was his only way to earn credits from ad-serves, although less all the time and now barely enough for food and filtered water.

He hustled to the bathroom to clean up. Crank, his mother's cat—now his, along with the house, since she'd passed last year—wound around his legs and bonked his shin.

"Yeah, I'm hungry, too."

Crank *merowed* his request again.

"I could get something from the dispensary, but you know how that went last time."

Rrow-row, Crank insisted. Being a ginger, he was stubborn.

"Alright, but you asked for it—"

An ad snatched away his attention, blaring across all his senses. *Your brightest smile for a brilliant day!*

He did his best to absorb it. The jingle played, a heart-rending story about toothpaste. The machine sucked in every response: heartrate, pupil dilation, hormones, even his old e-skin implant spooled off information. He didn't have credits to buy the product. At his index, he only got test-marketing ad serves, and his data was worth less every day. But this ad might generate enough credits to feed Crank, maybe him too. It wasn't fair: any mid-indexer could pay for a full meal with a single ad. But their attention was worth something. *They* were worth something.

When it finished, his dashboard said he'd lost half a credit for "distraction." *Dammit.* He knew better than to *think* during an ad. Only Crank would eat tonight.

He checked his shirt—not too wrinkled—and hurried to the front door. The only place in town he could holo-project for the date was a charge station that was an hour's walk, and that was just a pitstop for travelers. Most residents in the area had died or left. He'd worked at the last local job, a gun shop that burned down right after he'd moved back to care for his mom. The water was poison, the air was worse, and the soil was dead. No one stayed if they had a choice. He'd inherited the house, but you couldn't sell property in a pollution ghetto.

He could leave, but the only jobs were zero-index

—plague-ward nurse, sex worker, snuff filter for the data stream—and those only killed you faster with more misery. So he stayed and watched his index slowly spiral down.

He kept his walking pace steady. Didn't want to end up sweaty. Lilac would notice. She had to be higher-index than him—everyone was—and that might spook her. Not that they would actually pair up. But if they did, it would drag down her index... and pull up his. She might think that was *why* he wanted to meet, real faces. But it wasn't.

He told himself that a hundred times. He was pretty sure it was true.

Meeting in-holo *and* in-game meant more time together, without affecting anyone's index. She seemed like she wanted that. He knew he did. Tonight, he might get to know her real name, but he had to be careful.

The station was a blazing beacon of light, with its glowing chargers and ever-scrolling ads. The door's rusty hinges screamed from disuse, and the dispensary inside maybe got stocked once a quarter. Only a fool would drink the coffee.

He slid into place at the small table right as it came alive with her call. The top half of her—the part captured by holo—shimmered into relief. Long brown hair, pale face, teeth worrying her bottom lip.

"Hey," he breathed, still a little winded.

"Hey, yourself." Her eyes were wide, already spooked. He scanned her face for a reason why, but got lost in her softness—open expression, deep brown eyes, a tiny crease in her forehead. She seemed carefully treading unknown waters.

It drew him straight in. "This isn't fair."

"What's not fair?" The crease deepened.

That you're so obviously high index. "You didn't tell me you were beautiful."

"I'm not—you don't have to say that. You've seen me farm, Tripp."

"I've seen you *try* to farm." He couldn't stop the smile and sure didn't want to. "My name's Matthew, by the way. Matt, to my friends." He didn't have friends. Just her.

One heartbeat. Two. She chewed her lip furiously.

"It's okay. You don't have to—"

"Sara." She gulped in some air. "My name's Sara."

His smile would break his face. "Nice to meet you, Sara."

"This is so weird."

"Weird *nice,* though, right?"

"Yeah. I just..." She wound hair around one finger,

a tourniquet of tension. "I don't do this kind of thing."

"Holo dates?"

"Any dates."

"Me either." It felt like falling, his whole body cranked with tension then suddenly released. Even better than in-game. "We can take this slow. You don't have to—" The ad whipped his attention, leaving the words in his mouth. *It's a miracle cleaner for your toilet!* Images and a screech of song. *No, no, no.* But he couldn't stop it. He'd lost that privilege when he authorized auto-serve for credits he desperately needed. He couldn't do anything but react and wait... wait until the ad finished destroying the one good thing he had left...

It ended with a flourish. The look on Sara's face gutted him.

"You're on auto-serve." Her voice had gone flat.

"No, I just... forgot to turn it off..." A stupid thing to say. Only the lowest indexed ever turned on auto-serve. It was one step up from snuff-filtering.

"Don't lie to me." She was furious. And scared. And a dozen fleeting emotions he couldn't identify.

He reached out to her holo. "I can explain—"
But she was gone.

His hand dropped to the table. His insides were as empty as the nothingness she left behind.

One ad serve... and it was all gone.

They'd been doomed from the start. He should have kept it in-game. He was a fucking *idiot*. He wanted to pound the table and throw chairs, but he barely had energy to shuffle to the dispensary. He spent the ad credits on a tin of fake sardines for Crank.

It took far longer than an hour to drag himself home. When he reached the house, his index had dropped even further, penalizing him for the failed social encounter.

"It wasn't even a real date!" he screamed into the dark. He collapsed into the upholstered chair, the one his mom had used in the last stages of her dying. It embraced him like a tomb. Two more ads served, but he was numb. Eventually, a dull ache at his hip made him move. It was the fake fish.

"Crank! I brought you food."

He roused to look for the cat.

Crank was gone. His concern escalated when he found the back door had been pried open. *The hell?* But Crank had a tracker, left over from when his mom had extra credits. The account was still active, but the free version only tracked within two miles, and Crank was off the map.

It was too much to deal with. Hunger ravaged him. He grabbed a fork, forced down half the sardines, then sagged into the chair. Sleep took him before he could think about what to do next.

A barrage of ads hounded him: *cars he could never afford, handbags that cost a year's worth of food, a glittering diamond collar Crank would sooner piss on than wear.* An alarm jolted him awake. Auto-serve was supposed to shut off when you slept, but his dash had fresh credits. What was the point of serving ads to an unconscious mind? Must be some new test, trying to seep in to people's minds to make them buy stuff.

He checked what triggered the alarm: *Crank was back on the map.* Location: the back door. But when he stumbled to let the cat in, the bottom dropped out of his stomach. Crank had bandages where a cat-sized implant had been freshly installed, above his right eye.

Fucking hell. Someone was making money off his cat.

"Oh, bud, I'm sorry." He picked up Crank and stroked his non-bandaged cheek. The *mew* was quiet, but the rumble purr was loud. He carried Crank to the chair. "You're probably worth more than I am now." What ad would you serve a cat? It had to be some kind of testing. *Experimentation.* Whatever it was, Crank deserved better. He sure as hell wasn't letting someone torture his cat. "I'll figure out how to fix this, okay?"

Crank nibbled at the half tin of fish. There was only one vet he could find that worked outside the city, and they'd gone out of business. Or died. He turned to darker corners, bio-hacking channels, and made contact with someone named MeatDexD who agreed to meet him at the charger station. It took twenty minutes to rig a sling for Crank out of an old sheet, then an hour to hike back to the station. MeatDexD had gotten there first, judging by the solarbike charging outside.

Inside, a short woman had propped her boots on the table. "Took you long enough." Her head was shaved, with a tuft of feathers grafted at the front. The elaborate eye makeup and feather eyelashes made her look half owl.

"I don't have a bike. Had to walk."

She scowled. "Pay is half up front, half when the patient regains consciousness."

Crank made a well-timed complaint.

She dropped her boots to the floor and beckoned him over. He unbundled the sheet, and it draped like a tablecloth with Crank in the center.

"What the fuck did they do to you?" She said it soft, scratching Crank under his chin as she inspected the bandage. He slitted his eyes, leaning into her hand. "I hate people."

That didn't seem to require a response.

"I can remove the implant and stitch him up for free—because fuck whoever did this." She peered past her feather eyelashes. "But the drug to knock him out will cost you a hundred credits. Can't help that. It's tough to get." She stared at him, waiting. She had to know he didn't have it.

"I'll take some debt."

Her eyes widened. "You sure about that?"

His hand shook as he swiped the payment to her. His dash blared blood-red negative numbers.

"All right." She set to work, digging out tools from her bag, using a patch on Crank so his cat puddled into the table, unconscious well before she pulled apart the bandages.

He looked away, trying to clear his head. *A hundred credits of debt.* He'd starve before he made that back on ads. If he could even get served.

The surgery didn't take long, but Crank would be out for a while. The woman helped bundle up the cat, then offered a lift back to his place. She didn't want Crank pulling out his stitches. He was extra careful on the ride and as he dismounted from the bike.

"Hey." She flipped up her visor. "Whoever did this

will come looking for my orange boy. Lock your doors."

He nodded. "Thanks."

She sped off, leaving him to his dark house, a passed-out cat, and an insurmountable amount of debt. As he unbundled Crank and eased into the chair, cat nestled in his lap, the impossibility of it settled on him like a shroud. He was zero-index now, and no one worked their way out of that. The zero-indexed spent their credits on suppressors to get through the day. Eventually, the work ground you into oblivion. That was his future... but what about Crank?

He sank deeper into the chair. The soft glow of the city turned the walls silver.

An ad jolted him, although the music and visuals were gauzy and soft. *The Life Advantage Plan: a great way to give the ones you love the security they need!* He tried to pay attention, but he was tired. An older man hugged his family. Left on some kind of trip. Arrived at a brightly lit facility with kind-faced people. The music swelled as the man tapped his temple to activate his implant and then went into a trance. Smiling. The family gathered around a picture of him, teary eyed but grateful. Each had something new: a solarbike, education credits, a holiday feast that could feed dozens. *When you're ready to give the final gift, make it count.*

The ad faded.

It wasn't until the tiny credit for the ad appeared in his dash that he saw the message—*Subject to contract acceptance*—and a second vastly bigger credit —*pending*—that would wipe out his debt by a factor of ten. He sat up straighter, opened the message, scanned it quickly, and... he wasn't dying. But if he were, he could sign up to spend his final days in a flurry of ad-testing and suppressor-joy that would transport him into the Great Beyond... and leave his heirs with a tidy sum to compensate them for their loss.

Win, win.

He stared at the contract and its terrible offer. What tests would you run on the dying? Probably anything went—it wasn't like the dead could complain. Still, an idea crept into his mind like a shadow. Enough suppressors would kill anyone, whether you were dying or not. And it was painless, unlike every other option before him that involved living. He could set up something *safe* for Crank, away from where everyone was dying anyway, just slower and uglier.

He scratched Crank's ear. It'd been reckless to go into debt, but freeing Crank was the one good thing he'd managed to do in a long time. His life had been one long spiral down the index. For once, he'd pushed back the darkness, even though it had cost him everything. Strangely, that made it matter more. He wanted to see it through. *Make it count.*

It was freedom for both of them.

Signing the contract was easy. Setting up a lifetime account at the closest cat rescue was even easier, especially when he saw the name of the person running it.

The suppressors triggered as soon as the ad-serves started.

He petted Crank one last time. And then he felt nothing at all.

THE LAST THING Sara expected to find at her rescue pickup was Matt.

His eyes were open but unfocused with the look of someone blissed out on suppressors. Her charge, a ginger named Crank, nestled in a sheet on his lap.

Shock made her stupid for a moment, then she checked Matt's pulse. Weak but still there. She quickly called in an emergency shutoff of the suppressors, using up a rash of credits, but she didn't care. Matt's eyes drifted shut, and she couldn't wake him. He needed medical care, but no one came out here.

Guilt swam through her panic. The cat was bandaged, the house was falling down, and Matt's index, which she'd accessed during the emergency call, told a story all its own. Her freak-out about the auto-serve on their date—her panic that his low index might bring scrutiny she couldn't afford—came at the end of that story, but she was still part of it.

She bundled up Crank, who was groggy, and got him safely to the transport van. She hesitated longer than she wanted to admit... then went back for Matt.

"I DON'T UNDERSTAND why you bother." Alicia, a shelter volunteer, cringed at the sight of Matt, propped in the main room, surrounded by cats sunning themselves and perched on horizontal surfaces, including his lap. His IV line snaked up the pole to keep the cats from bringing the whole thing down.

"He won't be here much longer." Sara hated how that sounded defensive.

Alicia did her tour of duty with the litter boxes and left. Sara finished the afternoon feeding. She was washing up when an ad offer came through. She thought about refusing the offer, but turning it down would be suspicious, and the credits would pay for tomorrow's kibble. She authorized it to play. *Keep your pet trim and healthy with Perfect Pet! The only food matched to your pet's unique DNA.*

She lingered at the bathroom mirror, looking for what Matt saw in her. He didn't know about her auntie with the foresight to hoard real money and set up a shelter to launder it. Auntie Carol didn't foresee an economy controlled by credits and the index, but she knew a dark time was coming, when a low profile and stash of funds might be the difference between running a cat shelter and being a zero-index worker with no options worth living for.

Another ad request came through. Unusual to have them so close. She approved it. *Worried about the future? Get security for you and your loved ones with Credit Insurance. You'll never have to worry about—*

"Fuck! You!" She jabbed away the ad. She'd love to rip out her implant, if that wouldn't give away everything, her whole life of hiding in plain sight just to exist. A life that couldn't let anyone in except an anonymous friend in a fantasy game.

She pressed both palms to the mirror, gripping the edge and wanting to rip it from the wall. The system was always watching, always ready to hit you at your absolute lowest point.

She waited until the feeling of coming unglued passed. Then she wiped her eyes and returned to the main room, pulling up a chair next to Matt. She lifted one of his hands to pet the gray tabby curled on his lap.

She tapped her implant to join the game.

"Hey, there you are." Tripp sat on the deck of the farmhouse, hair tousled, like he'd just woken up.

"Hey, yourself." She gathered up a ribble and parked it on her shoulder. "I was thinking about those peaches. Might need some harvesting."

"Yeah, probably. I'm kinda beat, though." It was a miracle he could access the game. Each day she came back, she wasn't sure if he'd be here.

"I can do it for you." She snagged a bucket from the porch. "You rest up. I'll be right back."

"Hey, are we still on for tonight?" His smile ripped right through her.

"Yeah. Absolutely. Wouldn't miss it for the world."

"Me too." He relaxed into the chair. "Maybe leave some of those peaches for the buccas."

"Buccas gotta eat too."

"I'll be here when you get back."

There was no crying in the game.

She felt the wetness down her cheeks all the same.

Closet Full of Time

The Everything Machine

W e'll start by assuming I'm not crazy.

The tomatoes on my balcony were blooming when it first happened. I spent my time watching the world and living inside my books. I've read countless, even more since retiring from the library. George kept me company, as creaky in his seventeen cat years as me in my eighty human ones. My body obeyed the commands of gravity and age, but my mind was still sharp.

Or so I thought, until the Red Kid walked down my street.

I observed all the regulars from my fourth floor garden. Mr. Cho and his flower shop across the street. Tiny Mrs. Rabinowitz with her even tinier dogs. The street sweepers and delivery people, the schoolkids in their uniforms, the trio of men who gather on Saturday nights to sing. Then, in the quiet of mid-afternoon on a Tuesday, the Red Kid walked down my car-less street. Head-to-toe in shiny synthetic fabric, stretching over their whole body, making it impossible to see their face: just angular bones and gangly limbs and feet like puppy paws they haven't grown into. The audacity and absurdity of that young stride: you couldn't miss them. Even George poked his ginger nose between the balcony rails and sniffed.

They were gone in a minute, round a corner.

My old bones went inside and dug my tablet out of the drawer. I kept it there because I understood the Everything Machine, how it couldn't be trusted, and that was the best place for it. But sometimes I wanted something I couldn't get from the library that still sits uptown, a bus ride into the past, and I used the machine. My curiosity had always earned me trouble, and now it has me looking for the Red Kid on street cams and socials.

There was nothing.

I should have known then, but I didn't. I thought maybe Red Kid's costume had anti-detection built in, not that I'd misplaced trust, believing the machine dutifully recorded reality, despite knowing better. So I brought it to the balcony and placed it on my stack of old faithfuls—*1984*, *Handmaid's Tale*, and *Small Gods* because there was nothing in life a Terry Pratchett book couldn't make better. The machine defiled my small shrine, but that was less important than recording Red Kid's second appearance, in which I had an unnatural faith.

I waited.

I was halfway through a novel about the regenerative farming in the 30's when Red Kid showed up again in the empty street of mid-afternoon. They danced this time, a graceless bumpy stumble, and I recorded it all, smile wide on my face. Even George was excited, his tail quivering. Mr. Cho stepped outside with a bucket of daisies and stared.

I showed George the replay, but he'd been captured by a beam of sun, living out his best cat life. It'd been a while, but I figured out how to upload the recording, then I made some tea and dove back into the novel. By the time a storm forced me off the balcony—I brought in the shrine, George, and the machine—I finally remembered to check the results.

Everything was gone. The recording from my tablet, the upload, the posts. I sank deep into my comfortable chair, the one that reclines, where I sometimes sleep. I thought the senility had finally crept in, delivering hallucinations instead of memory gaps.

I shoved the machine back in the drawer.

I wanted to ask Mr. Cho, but I didn't. Instead, I waited until the shudder eased out of my body and told myself it would all go away, if I ignored it hard enough.

It wasn't my proudest moment.

Days passed before it happened again. So many days, I almost forgot it. I was tending my tomatoes when Red Kid appeared. Only this time they were running. So fast on those gangly legs, but not fast enough. Two enforcement officers closed in and fired that device, the one with strings that fingered the air and wrapped around people, making them twitch. I watched, heart in my feet, as they picked up Red Kid and dragged their limp body away.

George meowed. I shushed him.

I know what this is, and it's not me being crazy. I know before I check the machine, but I do it just to be sure: Red Kid has been rendered invisible to the world, *erased,* like before. That kid doesn't fit. I don't know exactly why, but I know if the machine is erasing someone, that someone needs to be seen. It takes me a minute, some strong tea, and an hour with Pratchett to decide. Then more time to dig out that quilt I never finished, the one with extinct birds on each square. I don't have time to stitch—there's no time, not anymore—so I rummage some fabric and glue.

Then I write a note for Maria, my neighbor who helps me with groceries. I tell her to take the tomatoes and ask her to find a good home for George. I give him all the treats I have left, in a bowl on the balcony, while I hang my banner.

I Saw Red Kid, it declares.

If I'm crazy, I guess nothing will happen.

But if I'm not, maybe someone else will see the Everything Machine takes more than it gives. That our trust in its performance of wisdom is misplaced. All it can ever encode is *us* and our flaws, and a pale copy at that. I've spent so long in this place where the plants grow green and the people live in analog time, I'd almost forgotten the machine reaches even here. That people trust the wrong thing, doubt the wrong folks, find reasons to look away, even me. I forgot we have no built-in radar for truth. It has to be shouted at us from the 4th floor in bright red letters.

Even then, we allow the possibility of knowing to be erased.

I pick up *Small Gods* and keep company with Terry, as I wait for them to come get me.

Closet Full of Time

In the end, it was the loneliness that broke us.

I remember the time before the closet, before you fell in love with it. You'd been obsolesced out of two industries already, landing in care work with me, but you didn't like the papery skin of the elderly or how their minds skipped tracks, so you grabbed the closet with both hands. Not literally—you stepped through the doorway—but you know what I mean.

Back then, it was easy to understand the desire to retreat. The world was in a hyperactive race, and no one could keep up. Humanity's collective power had been harnessed to an inhuman drive, always pressing forward, untethered from wisdom and compassion. The future rushed at us like a driving snowstorm, obscuring everything and forcing us to shelter our eyes from the onslaught of bitter ice. We were stuck in the tiny tricycle of our human chassis, furiously pumping our tired legs while going nowhere. We felt frozen, unable to change anything, even as change happened frenetically all around us.

Escape into the closet made perfect sense. (And yet I still didn't go.) Who wouldn't want to step out of the storm into a protected little box where you'd be given a moment to warm your heart again? To unfreeze the rigor mortis of fear and have the refuge of human speed? Or simply to rest. We were being constantly etched away by a world that simply swept the remains of us back into the grinder.

When you came back from the closet, you were refreshed, happier. You felt safer in there. Who could argue with that? We argued anyway. Wasn't I supposed to be your safe harbor? But how do I protect you from a world trying to eat you, piece by piece?

Then you slipped away again into that pocket space, a gift given to us by ourselves, the one invention among the endless stream that finally allowed a real reprieve: step into the box and you stepped outside of time. A cosmic time-out room where your body remained but your mind dilated. A thousand seconds or minutes or days—your choice, always yours—a massive headtrip squeezed between one heartbeat and the next. Your body didn't go anywhere, just stepped into the closet, closed the door, activated the link, and an instant later, you're done. But inside your mind, a week had lolled by of leisurely reading and movie-watching and playing in virtual worlds.

I stayed outside, with the dying and not-yet-dying.

You came back changed. For you, the world had slowed down, a single moment stretched into days. For me, it kept speeding up.

"I'm adapting," you said.

"You're cheating," I snapped. But I didn't say with whom or what.

To be clear, I knew no one was in there with you. The technology simply wasn't built for two: you couldn't force someone into a closet that interfaced with your mind and demanded consent. It was foolproof that way, which we knew because a lot of fools tried. No one else could sync into that tiny slice of real time to live the days and weeks with you. You were alone with the machine, an intimate solo affair of the senses, but yours alone.

I began to think of time as your mistress. *Jealous* wasn't quite the right word, but close. It stabbed another tiny hole in my pincushion heart each time you announced you were popping into the closet for a "refresh."

It got worse. More times each month, then each week. Soon, it was once a day. You stopped telling me when you'd gone. Or for how long.

There was a price, of course. You paid for your peace in days, sometimes weeks, subtracted from your lifespan. Some fools stepped into the closet forever and turned to ash. Your body might not need to eat or pee during the small slice of real time in the closet, and maybe a cancer couldn't grow in that tiny moment, but you aged all the same. It took a lot of energy to run the machine—and dilate a brain—and that didn't come for free. Quantum computers gorged on energy to keep up with the humans stepping out of time. At least the machines ran on clean electrons from the sun —environmental advocates proclaimed it the lowest carbon existence —but the finite resource that got consumed was *you*. Each day you spent in closet time extracted a day from your telomeres and vitality. You aged an equivalent amount, only instantaneously, at least as seen by those outside the box. Entropy got its due, no matter what, mainlining the energy of youth straight out of your veins.

There was no cheating reality. You slowed down by racing ahead.

"We've become a May-December romance," I joked.

"Don't be age-ist," you snapped.

One day, the world was too much even for me, and I stepped into the closet. I hoped it would bring us back together, two records skipping the same tracks. If I caught up to you, maybe our worlds would fall in sync once more.

I expected white space and numbness but found a virtual world almost as alive as the real one. I poked at shows, the vast library of entertainment created before that moment in normal time, bingeing all 7 seasons of *How to Hate Your Ex,* a rumination that was probably unhealthy, but what did that mean when your body still awaited the next heartbeat?

I left when I couldn't stand the isolation any more. Emerging from the closet was like escaping a simulation only to find the real world had flattened as well. I understood less, not more, how this invention was supposed to be an adaptation to a world moving at hyper speed.

I wasn't refreshed. I was haunted. I vowed never to go back in.

We were now permanently on opposites sides of the glass from each other.

Then the most predictable thing happened, yet still surprised everyone: *the closet changed.* Suddenly, you could sync up with someone else in the box. Not physically, of course, none of this involved the body, but that hardly mattered with the rapid acceleration of sensory inputs and cortical dilators and other words that meant nothing to me except I was losing you more.

This was no longer about a time-out, a chance to adjust to the world's dizzying change. Now it was about creating a new world, a preferable world.

People stopped coming back.

Voluntary, always voluntary. Some wanted this, *needed* it, and how could you argue with that? You didn't, but I did. How was escape voluntary when we'd made the world unlivable? How was this optional when the world wore you down to a nub, used you up only to toss you aside for someone fresh, someone who had *adapted* to the inhuman pace, ready to be newly fed into the grinder?

"It's not sustainable," I said.

"I'm leaving," you responded.

The only surprise was how unsurprised I was. That they'd invented a way to take someone into the closet, and you didn't want to take me. Not that I would have gone. But you were ready to go so easily without me.

I noticed a new white hair woven into your blond ones. I said nothing. We were hardly speaking. What was there left to say? I hoped she would treat you well?

That you would be good to each other in there? I couldn't voice the horror I really felt.

You didn't leave right away.

You went to the park, visited friends, shopped the farmer's market and bought out the flower stand. You filled our home with them. *It's like a funeral,* I didn't say. You were saying goodbye, but not to me: to the world.

And then you were standing awkward in front of the closet. You said you were sorry, but it was better this way. For both of us.

I stayed mute. You were about to step off a cliff, and there were no words that would stop it, only ones that would make it worse.

Then you stepped through, and by the time I was brave enough to look, you'd returned to stardust and memories. A long, full life gone between heartbeats, mine and yours.

A few people still stepped into the closet for a day or two, only to find an empty graveyard. Your presence —*your absence*—was overwhelmingly stamped upon both worlds. The time closets slowly shut down. Turned out companies closed pretty quickly when most of the customers had become ash.

I put you on a shelf, in a beautiful earthen vase that my beloved, another closet widow, had made for you.

My beloved and I whispered sweet reassurances that we made the right choice, that here was real and there was not. None of it mattered except now and now and now.

But in reality: those piles of dust you all left behind broke us.

It took time and a lot of anger for me to forgive you: to understand that some hearts are punctured too easily in a world made of needles and the fault lies with the needles, not the tender flesh. You made your world human again because we refused to make ours safe for you.

I was slow: many figured it out before me.

That we'd been locked in cages of loneliness, and we had to break out, smash the hold a million things had on us, most of all the belief that we needed more than we already had. We figured out how to change the world so it fit human bodies and human minds, rather than force minds and bodies to fit an inhuman world.

You broke us in a way that finally let new things in.

That was when the unfolding began.

I wish you could see us now, ten years on, the child we made, the strong and healthy one you refused to bring into the harsh inhuman world. If we had all chosen to leave, as you did, we wouldn't have this world. And we wouldn't have it if you'd stayed, either.

I had been right: *it wasn't sustainable.* And you were right too: *you adapted.*

So I watch the dust dance in the sun and pet the cat and think how madness is being alone, and we were all so mad for so long, insanity became the norm. We had to reinvent human time, rediscover the infinite seconds inside lovemaking and window gazing. We didn't have to stop time to make human time; we had to be human inside the time we had.

What needed fixing, all along, was us.

Maybe, in closet time, you were able to invent everything you needed between heartbeats. Maybe you found a thousand nows inside one frozen second of eternity.

I hope so, with all my punctured heart.

A Note From Sue

It was very soon after the debut of generative AI tools for creating images and text that I was confronted with a choice: **did I want a story of mine associated with an AI-generated image?**

The stakes were relatively high: this was one of my first sales to a professional Sci-Fi zine, and taking a stand might mean losing publication. It was also early days, chatGPT had just been released, and it wasn't clear (yet) how much theft had occurred and how much damage would be done. How many artists and narrators would lose their jobs, how many writers would simply quit in despair of the devaluation of their art. This was before AI submissions shut down Clarkesworld, showing how wildcard the impacts from AI scams would be.

I had to make a choice: **I told the publisher I would rather pull my story than publish it with an AI image.** That I knew artists impacted by this and it wasn't right. They didn't agree, but they were willing to retract the image and still publish my story.

Months later, I had to make that same choice again, in a similar situation. After that, I made sure not to submit to anyone unless they had an explicit anti-AI policy, which thankfully was the direction the majority of the industry soon moved.

I went on to write anti-AI editorials and blog posts. I contacted politicians and spoke out. I championed the lawsuits against OpenAI and the social rejection of AI images and text and voice narration. I fought AI usage wherever I could and doubled down on hiring (more) human artists and narrators.

The assault on the arts continues.

As will my resistance.

But through it all, being a writer, I have been observing what's happening—to the technology, to our culture, to our minds, bodies, and souls—and I have a lot of thoughts.

And writers turn thoughts into stories.

These stories were born out of that chaotic early time when the technology was new and the social disruption fresh. The strident insistence that AI adoption in everything was "inevitable" was the hype that fueled a hundred venture capitalists' and tech optimists' dreams, but it was never reality: reality was the degradations and harms—to people and the environment—that had already occurred and are ongoing. Reality was that you can't un-ring the bell of inventing something that is "a lying machine made out of crimes"— especially while so many are still trying to recoup their massive investment in it.

But I think genAI was a turning point, and not in the way the enthusiasts expected: it was the first time in my living memory (and I predate the internet) that a technology was so shiny at first and yet so utterly rejected by so many so quickly. We're starting to wake up to the darker side of technology. You can tell the tech optimists have burnt through their good will when the term Luddite starts getting reclaimed.

This collection of stories is my attempt to say "this won't stop where you think it should, this will keep going, if we allow it." These stories are the Black-Mirror-opposite of my solarpunk and hopepunk tales (you can even see that alternate green world peeking through), and that's not by accident.

The choice before us is increasingly between those two poles: regeneration or degradation. Human or anti-human. Sustainable or continue burning through the planet as if we don't live on it.

I had to make a choice early on and there was never really any doubt: I choose humanity and arts and sustainability and life.

It's a little deceiving to even say there's a choice: the danger has always been—and continues to be—that the thing the machines (all our inventions, all our hubris) will consume is us.

In Hope (even in the dark),

Sue

HALFWAY TO BETTER

Hopeful Solarpunk Anthology

A collection of short stories, each exploring a near-future where we're struggling to survive the climate crisis and build a better world.

Get the collection or download the first story, *Slimy Things Did Crawl,* for free:

SLIMY
THINGS DID CRAWL
SUSAN KAYE QUINN

My *Nothing is Promised* series is complete.

My favorite review of this series from @scavello:

"I recently read the Nothing is Promised series by fedi's own @susankayequinn and really enjoyed it. It's a solar/hope punk series that I've been describing as a fun flirty gay scooby gang solving a power grid mystery."

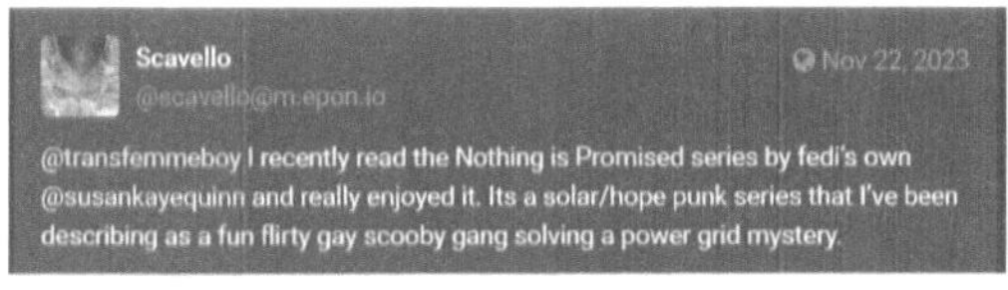

NOTHING IS PROMISED

Hopepunk Climate Fiction

In a world beset with climate-driven plagues, power engineer Lucía Ramirez just wants a family to join...but she finds a mystery on Power Island One instead.

NOTHING IS PROMISED

Hopepunk Climate Fiction

In a world beset with climate-driven plagues, power engineer Lucía Ramirez just wants a family to join…but she finds a mystery on Power Island One instead.

Book 1, Book 2, Book 3, Book 4

HALFWAY TO BETTER

Solarpunk

A collection of short stories, each exploring a near-future world where we're struggling to survive the climate crisis and build a better world.

SINGULARITY

Hopepunk Sci-Fi

Eli is a legacy human, preserved for his genetic code, but he would give anything to ascend with the rest of humanity.

MINDJACK

YA Sci-Fi

When everyone reads minds, a secret is a dangerous thing to keep.

ROYALS OF DHARIA

Alt-India Steampunk Romance

The Third Daughter of the Queen must go undercover as the fiancé of a barbarian prince to find a weapon of war.

DEBT COLLECTOR

Cyberpunk

When your debts exceed your potential life earnings, debt collectors come take your life energy and give it to someone more "worthy."

FAERY SWAP

Middle Grade Fantasy

Finn becomes stuck the Otherworld when a runaway faery prince steals his body.

Most of SKQ's books are available in audiobook.

Get a free box set of Singularity novellas when you subscribe to SKQ's Newsletter.

About the Author

Susan Kaye Quinn is a PhD Environmental Engineer turned speculative fiction author and the host of *Bright Green Futures,* a podcast that lifts up stories about a more sustainable and just world. Sue writes hopeful climate fiction, futuristic spec fic, cyberpunk, and steampunk romance. Her novels have been optioned for Virtual Reality and translated into German and French, while her short stories have been published by *Grist, Little Blue Marble, Reckoning* and more. Sue believes being gentle and healing is radical and disruptive. She writes full-time, trying to build a better world by imagining it first.

Website: SusanKayeQuinn.com

Podcast/substack: BrightGreenFutures.wtf